The Funny Bunny Fly

The Funny Bunny Fly

**Written and
Illustrated by**

Bethany Straker

**Sky Pony Press
New York**

Once upon an apple pie,
there was a Funny Bunny Fly.
It sat and slurped the sticky juice,
until it turned a shade of puce.

It fatly struggled to the floor
and shoved itself under the door.
I'm hot, it thought. And so it flew
upon some nearby dog doo-doo.

It wriggled in the cooling mess,
in stinky goo its ears were pressed.
The Bunny Fly flew loop the loop
and sprayed a waterfall of poop.

A bakery sat on the hill,
the fresh-baked smells would float and fill
the Funny Bunny's twitchy nose
of cakes and biscuits, I suppose.

Once inside, it was a dream,
a cave of chocolate, jam, and cream!
It plunked itself on sticky tart,
the sugared sweetness swelled its heart.

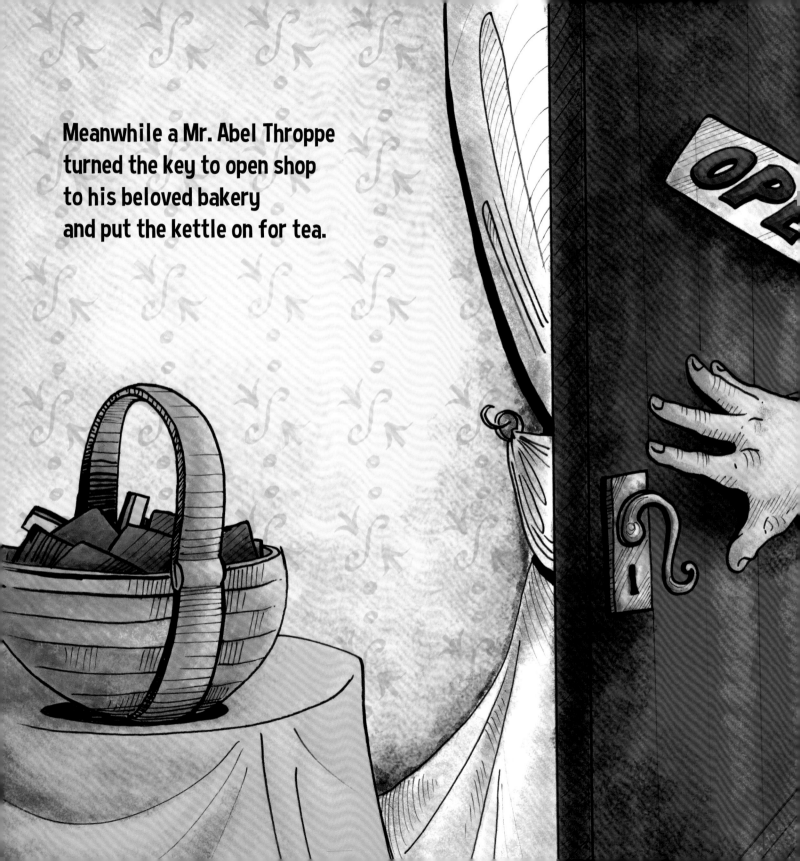

Meanwhile a Mr. Abel Throppe
turned the key to open shop
to his beloved bakery
and put the kettle on for tea.

A jingle jangle of the bell
and Mr. Throppe arose to sell
his finest cakes, his finest bread,
to hungry shoppers—get them fed.

"I'd like a sticky tart to eat,"
said Mrs. Button. "What a treat!"
Our Bunny Fly had left the plate
but left a mess—oh no! too late!

She got the tart under her arm.
The stinky poop would do her harm!
She trotted off to have a drink
and cut a slice and have a think.

And all the while inside the shop,
the Funny Bunny Fly did flop
and laze about on all the food,
upon it doggie poop now glued.

Twenty customers that day
bought a cake or chocolate tray.
All but two went home that night,
their tummies feeling not quite right.

BANG BANG BANG! upon the door
the morning after, at the store.
"You made us sick! You horrid man!"
"You pay us back or face a ban!"

The saddest part was Throppe knew why,
as later on he saw the fly.
"I'll pay them back. I won't be mean,
and from now on I'll keep it clean!"

The moral is to keep things clean.
We all must have tip-top HYGIENE.
Wash your hands, and don't touch poop,
or you'll be sorry—there's the scoop!

Sky Pony Press books may be purchased in bulk at special discounts for sales promotion, corporate gifts, fund-raising, or educational purposes. Special editions can also be created to specifications. For details, contact the Special Sales Department, Sky Pony Press, 307 West 36th Street, 11th Floor, New York, NY 10018 or info@skyhorsepublishing.com.

Sky Pony® is a registered trademark of Skyhorse Publishing, Inc.®, a Delaware corporation.

Visit our website at www.skyponypress.com.

10 9 8 7 6 5 4 3 2 1

Manufactured in China, July 2014
This product conforms to CPSIA 2008

Library of Congress Cataloging-in-Publication Data is available on file.

Cover design by Danielle Ceccolini
Cover illustration by Bethany Straker

Print ISBN: 978-1-62914-610-2
Ebook ISBN: 978-1-63220-209-3